THE HORROR WRITERS ASSOCIATION PRESENTS

POETRY SHOWCASE
VOLUME III

Edited by

DAVID E. COWEN

Horror Writers Association

2016

Horror Writers Association Presents Poetry Showcase Volume III

ISBN 978-0-9858089-4-5

First Edition

For information please contact Horror Writers Association, PO Box
56687, Sherman Oaks, CA 91413, U.S.A. or at hwa@horror.org

Please visit www.horror.org for more information on the Horror Writers
Association

HWA Poetry Showcase Volume I is available in e-book form from Amazon
and Kobo.

HWA Poetry Showcase Volume II is also available in e-book from Amazon and Kobo.

CONTENTS

Introduction

In 1721 Thomas Parnell ushered in the era of the "Graveyard Poets" also known as the "Bone Yard Boys" with his poem "A Night-Piece on Death", mesmerizing English readers with his dark musings on death:

When men my scythe and darts supply,

How great a King of Fears am I!

They view me like the last of things:

They make, and then they dread, my stings.

Fools! if you less provoked your fears,

No more my spectre-form appears.

Death's but a path that must be trod

With their dark poetry these Graveyard Poets helped to usher in the Romantic Period which gave birth to the "dark and stormy night" during the volcano induced "year without summer" when Mary Godwin (Shelley) took her turn at telling a dark tale to her friends Polidori, Bryon and Percy (Shelley) on the banks of Lake Geneva. Mary Shelley's *Frankenstein; or, The Modern Prometheus* and later Polidori's *The Vampyre*, both inspired by that night, helped to popularize the literary genre known as "horror."

From the ancient *Epic of Gilgamesh* to Lovecraft's *Yule Horror* ("There is death in the clouds") to modern classics such as Bram Stoker Award® winner *The Four Elements*, written by Linda Addison, Rain Graves, Charlee Jacob, and Marge Simon, dark poetry has walked side by side with dark fiction. Before the modern novel readers relished in delight at epic narrative poems of the dark and fantastical.

To honor this partnership of dark poetry and horror fiction and in celebration of National Poetry Month the Horror Writers Association commissioned a new competition in 2014 called the Horror Poetry Showcase. Peter Adam Salomon edited the first two volumes which were both Amazon bestsellers in several poetry related categories. Peter's work on those anthologies cemented dark poetry's place with the HWA.

In 2016 the HWA Horror Poetry Showcase was, for the first time, reserved strictly for members. Despite some nervousness that a more limited field would yield limited results, there was a tremendous breadth of themes and styles. The poems detail horrors on a scale from the cataclysmic down to the ordinary turned malicious and twisted. While honored that many of the great poets of the genre submitted entries, I am equally proud of those entries from authors who had never published a single poem previous. This Showcase is a trophy case of modern speculative poetry.

I want to thank jury members Stephanie Wytovich and John Palisano for the joy and energy they gave to this year's Showcase. At the outset we all agreed on one basic premise: the poems we selected for including in the

Showcase had to be good poetry. There is no "pass" for genre, only a reward for good writing. Picking the top poems amongst so many fine submissions was difficult. After a number of exchanges between us it is my pleasure to present the HWA Horror Poetry Showcase Volume III.

– David E. Cowen, Editor

The Juror's Notes

John Palisano.

So often I will meet people ... fans of the genre, even ... who are surprised when they learn there are still many people reading and creating new dark poetry. "You mean there's more than Poe? More than the stuff I read in high school?" With the current renaissance of amazing work in the horror literary field, its poets have been producing so much wonderful work that I'm thrilled to have helped select some of the best from the current crop of the HWAs top practitioners.

Stephanie Wytovich.

The poetry showcase is a wonderful addition to everything that the HWA already provides for its members, and its presence in the market is proof that poetry is alive and well. So often, I think that writers are afraid of the form because it's taught to us as children in such a structured format that it seems intimidating and inaccessible. What the HWA is doing here though, is allowing writers to experiment and explore with poetry to find new ways and avenues to tell the stories that they want to tell. It's promoting genre and creative growth, and it is my firm belief that writers need to constantly be honing their craft and reinventing their approach, and I think the showcase is a great example of how they can do that.

About the Judges for the Showcase

John Palisano is the winner of the 2016 Bram Stoker award for Superior Achievement in Short Story and a two-time Bram Stoker nominated author. His short fiction has appeared in venues such as the Lovecraft eZine, Horror Library, Terror Tales, and many more. His novel Nerves was released by Bad Moon Books. He is also a contributor to FANGORIA magazine. Check him out at: **www.johnpalisano.wordpress.com**.

Stephanie Wytovich is the Poetry Editor for Raw Dog Screaming Press, a book reviewer for Nameless Magazine, and a well-known coffee addict. She is a member of the Science Fiction Poetry Association, an active member of the Horror Writers Association, and a graduate of Seton Hill University's MFA program for Writing Popular Fiction. Her poetry collections, Hysteria: A Collection of Madness, Mourning Jewelry, and An Exorcism of Angels are all Bram Stoker Award-nominated, and her debut novel, The Eighth, will be out in 2015 from Dark Regions Press. Check out her website at **http://stephaniewytovich.blogspot.com**.

David E. Cowen is the author of "The Madness of Empty Spaces," (Weasel Press, November 2014) and the upcoming "Seven Yards of Sorrow" (Weasel Press September 2016). His other volume of poetry is entitled "Sixth and Adams" (PW Press 2001). His work has appeared in the 2014 and 2015 editions of the Horror Writers' Association's Horror Poetry Showcase, The Horror Zine, Literary Hatchet, Degenerates: Voices for Peace, "Dark Matter" (UH Downtown), Harbinger Asylum, AIPF's di-vêrsé-city Anthology, Texas Poetry Calendar, Isotropic Fiction

Magazine, the Canadian Broadcasting Company's Outfront Radio series and among many others. David's short story "Goth Thing," appeared in the award winning series, Exotic Gothic 5, Volume 1 published by PS Publishing. Other short stories have appeared in various journals including Haunted Traveler, Peripheral Distortions and The Dead Walk Anthology. Non-fiction articles and essays have appeared in CineAction (Canada's leading film magazine), ThisIBelieve.org's "On Motherhood", The Encyclopedia of the Zombie: The Walking Dead in Popular Culture and Myth and other journals. David is the president and a lifetime member of the Gulf Coast Poets Chapter of the Poetry Society of Texas. His website is at **www.decowen.com**.

Enough

When the surf turns to galloping steeds
thundering up and down the beach,
their pounding hooves throwing clots

of sand skyward, sending sunbathers
and families swollen with children
scurrying scared to their shiny cars,

when the arms of night are filled
with predatory birds who have
developed a taste for human flesh,

perched on church steeples, capitol
domes, mail boxes, parking meters,
awaiting those who prove unwary

enough to venture into the dark,
when trees from pole to pole and
continent to continent kamikaze

themselves on power lines and
pipelines, roadways and railway
tracks, leaving us shivering or

sweltering in our four walls,
when locusts swarm, plagues
thrive and mutate, typhoons

wail, oceans rise and overflow,
when nuclear reactors meltdown,
plastering the landscape with

a storm of radioactive debris,
when the Net collapses, virused
to oblivion, never to rise again,

when the Four Horsemen of
the Apocalypse come riding
out of the clouds, their ghastly

skulls bared and grinning,
scythes and swords flashing,
then at last we understand

that Earth has had its fill of
profligate madness and our
turn at the wheel has passed.

— *Bruce Boston*

Nuclear Winter Kiss

if a mushroom sprouts from the ground
        and stretches like a cloud
      does the blast still make a sound?

we relish in the contoured flesh
rough like a relief map
every crevice a newly excavated cavern
we decipher back braille
burns like brittle bark
professional prosthetics
we peel rubbery layers away
scrub off adhesive
rub the meat raw

our lips caress the burns
fallout numbs the nerves

fingers welded
hair   floating
   falling and
sculpted by male pattern baldness
ravaged by
radiation

rub the meat raw
deeply
sensually

crack and roll the tightened knots
bodies moaning like old ghosts

hopeless mutations, united in war
hollowed out husks of living char

are you my hometown
            hibakusha
            honey?

your one sullied eye
grub-white
soupy
begging for a spoon to be
                        dipped in it
                        scooped in it
let me taste your
        terrible
        tapioca

in the aftermath
the uncountable gray
we are
kissingandfuckingandpissingandcoupling
in spite of sterility
        of infertility
or
perhaps
in honor of these newfound blessings

— Chad Stroup

Always the Black and White Keys

The scent of absinthe incense lingers
From Brazil.
Of course I am a witch, raising the dead.
Come, I say, pulling at their clothing,
Wiping dirt from their bones.
They are no less alive than I.
Always lilies arrived from a stranger on a day of
heartbreak.

It was the season of resurrection
When my mother passed away.
The demarcation of sweet earth blooming,
Forsythia, cherry trees, magnolia
Against the pale horse of Death.
Always Spring arrived in a day of heartbreak.

I wait in a mirror for my mother to come,
Write a message in response with lipstick or eyeliner.
Always music dissolved me in days of heartbreak.
Always the black and white keys nailed me down.

– Corrine De Winter

Tea for Two

I didn't mean it.
really, I didn't.
not at all.
the poison, that is.
we were kids
playing.
tea party and all that.
I was so literal.
always.
so we couldn't have pretend tea.
I had to mix something.
there was this bag.
I didn't read what it was.
I was a kid.
kids don't read directions
or warnings.
I scooped some granules out
into the little teapot.
it was green.
the teapot.
the granules were white.
I poured a little water in.
I stirred and stirred.
then I poured the tea
into our green plastic cups.
and I told you, sternly,
don't drink this.
it's poison.
you looked at me
and smiled

and drank.
you always were a fool.
even when we were kids.
you didn't feel well after that
and ran home.
you had to go to the hospital.
to have your stomach pumped.
I told him not to drink it,
I said to my parents.
they nodded.
you were still my friend after that,
and we grew up
become lovers.
we lived together for years
then you drifted.
I cried.
you smiled.
I begged to you to come back.
you smiled.
we talked, and I cried more
and you returned home.
and it was all good
except for when it wasn't.
I always thought you were the fool.
no.
it was me.
you knew then you could do anything
anything to step on my heart.
anything.
I would beg you
beg you to come back.
I did.
time after time, year after year.

you're back again.
until the next time.
let's celebrate being together
because we are civilized
we can talk about anything, right?
anything.
have some tea.
here in this bone china cup
so delicate, so beautiful.
and I'm telling you now.
don't drink this tea.
don't.
really.
don't.
you're smiling again.
but so am I.

— *Kathryn Ptacek*

The Trappings of Poetry

My keyboard is a trigger pad.
I wait for just the right moment
and punch Ctrl+Alt+M --
capturing my goddess
of inspiration in a bear trap
made of whittled down typewriter keys
as sharp as a fistful of shanks.
She tries to crawl away
like a leg-broken dying dog
crooning something pained and panicky
like a clown blubbering bad poetry.
But the chain keeps her pegged
and she can only mope all bloody
spinning around in tedious circles
of increasing exhaustion going nowhere.
And after a while she finally gives up
and just glares at me, breathing heavy
like she can't dream without movement.
And we get into this staring match
that lasts as long as disease
and I'm surprised she doesn't even try
to chew her own leg off
or trick me into approaching.
She'd rather die
than give me any thrilling ideas now
but I know I can outlast her
and soon she blinks to sleep
like an animal that's just been injected.
And as I pensively watch her
beautiful body jerk to death
splashing spastically in
the inky puddle of her
muse ooze
I get this concept all over me

and I write.

– Michael A. Arnzen

Ant Farm Necropolis

A Plexiglas haze obstructs him
from life's cherished remnants.
Childhood treasures beckon
beneath a nebulous residue of dust.
Debased and diminished by addiction,
his ragged soul flees endless pursuit.
Death has swapped meth mites
for something more relentless.
Crumbling soil encroaches,
choking his spirit, hampering escape.
His consciousness, eternally fleeing,
races forward, freezes, doubles back.
Their goal: seize his essence,
mandibles will shred it to tatters.
As a child, he starved their ranks,
and tweezed their limbs.
Scorched them with match flame
and magnifying-glass glare.
Tortured and degraded
first them — now him.
Eternally, in earthen tunnels,
spectral formicary phantoms
exist to exact unending vengeance
in this ant farm necropolis.

— Adrian Ludens

The Ghost Subway

After having a few too many drinks
some claim that in the stomach of the city,
just below Joe's Bar
or perhaps in the cellar of the funeral store,
near the corner of Steinbeck Street,
the entrance of the Ghost Subway stands
the one with the blue wagons
decorated by the graffiti of fat pythons
and millions of photographs of black and white faces,
who carry the souls of the old ones
to the warehouse of the dead.

Some others say that the driver of that Subway is Tom Joad
with the brand new license of Charon in his pocket,
freed from his apartment in Hell thanks to a special permit,
and his wife, Rosa Tea
with her ivory wedding dress and a long train,
held up by two angels with useless hen's wings
wearing a blue T-shirt with CALIFORNIA written above,
she walks through the wagons to nurse the most tired
souls
with her compassionate breasts
swollen with cyanide.

The ticket of the Ghost Subway is free
and you don't have to look for its station,
it will find you when the time comes
when the rain fills your shoes and socks

and hundreds of snails crawl
on the edges of the old jar of your soul,
when you're too tired to die
and you need a ride to the other side, quickly
running under the belly of the indifferent buildings
which don't believe in ghosts.

And then there are those who tell the story
of the poet called Route 66
with the wool hat pulled down to his eyes
and the blue notebook in his jacket pocket
who discovered the Ghost Subway station
before he died, before all the others,
so he travels every night in those blue wagons
taking notes, heartening the frightened souls.
He reaches the other side and goes back to the city
to sit under the arcades, at the same place
to tell a thousand stories to the bystanders
who throw pennies into his hat.

— *Alessandro Manzetti*

Fragments from a Notebook in Hell

There would be ways to resolve
The human problem
As fancy dictates
Or engines design

A skull spattered with wordgore
Introduced cunningly beneath the skin
They'll barely feel it
And if ever, as a cooling sensation
As neurons spark and fade
Reborn immaculate
"We belong dead"

With pinpoint precision
We stab the universal retina
And all eyes weep the message
(Have a nice day)

Corpses culled afterward
Spun with viral weave
Green and bloated
As a frog's body
Shrinks to delicate bone

Enigmatic, ciphers to their minds
A touring faculty of brain-scribblers
Keeps the pace, one step ahead
Dabblers in deepest red

Fragments crumble, yellow pulp
Graffiti for cerebellar cities
We'll see you on your wedding night
Torches raised like the light of liberty
As the line to the castle winds
The mountain where it lies
Scored from within
With the cruelest music.

— Alex S. Johnson

Death Waits

He touched her cheek
and frowns to see
the age spots blossom
beneath his fingers.

He can't resist
just one more kiss
even though he knows
beneath his lips
hers wither.

Her eyes flutter open
lined but alive
clear and alert
full of passion.

"Are you ready now?"
he murmurs to her, hoping.

The sun spies from beneath the horizon
hiding beneath twilight linens
to hear what she might say.

She looks into her lover's eyes —
he cares for her, she knows —
but she is not yet ready to be his.

"Another day longer," she answers
and he sighs with longing.

The sun shrugs and begins
the ascent to morning.

"I will wait for you
as long as it takes then..."
and he retreats.

She rises to meet her day
taking Life in her hands
not quite ready to give up
that first love for him who waits.

Greying and wispy hair
floats from her as she exits
and he catches it with bony fingers —
snatching it from the air and sun —
to hold dear where he sits and pines.

Death waits patiently

— *Angela Smith*

The Shed

The lawn lays wide
and bright with yellow
sunshine, spread flat
with no corners,

except the shed.

The shed's paint is pale
but dull, like the owners
who inherited it
thought the best
they could do was make it
"blend in." And it does,
for a second

until your eyes catch
the black rectangle
of the haphazardly open doors
like they're stuck in their tracks
gummed up with debris putrefied
to the same color of black,
jarring in all that wide bright.

And you try not to picture what lies in there
what things might collect and colonize in a structure
so low and squat,
but there you go picturing centipedes
and scorpions, spiders and weevils, snakes and rats,
and other, darker things that can't be

– can't possibly be in that shed — yet there
you go picturing them: tentacles from corners
and tall, pale men standing against the walls,
and chittering, creeping things that slide down off the
ceiling and
open your doors at night, when they can't be seen,
but then then, that's not the most disturbing
part of that old shed.

The most disturbing part is how the structure itself seems
sly and sentient with its thin metal walls propped like
foldable gills, with its near-flat little roof peaks subtly like
an eyebrow, how its rotted wood floors lie in panels, like
they could all be rolled back like a tongue shoving food to
the gullet, how that open rectangle of black at the doors
sits still, patiently, waiting, and how eventually, when this
moment of feverish imagination has regressed under the
rightful armor of adulthood and you have nearly forgotten
all about it (nearly),
you will have to go inside it.

— *Annie Neugebauer*

Ghoul Mistress

One winter night I caught a glimpse of her.
Enwrapped in fog of ghostly, glowing green,
She followed in my wake, unheard, unseen.
Her icy, killing kisses had no cure.

She caught my eye and left the other fools,
For she had found the lover she desired.
Her eyes entrapped me, and I was admired;
I was her mortal, diamond of her jewels.

She drifted through the fog and drew so near,
Admiring me with greenish goblin-fires.
Without a word, she knew my dark desires;
She could unlock my most forbidden fears.

Before I said a single word, she kissed
My lips and stirred a storm of ice in me.
My skin grew cold, yet, dying, I was free.
My ghoulish mistress only would be missed.

— *Ashley Dioses*

3 AM at Clio's Laundromat

Wedged between the shadows of an alley
past the cold fire of the neon lights,
where the country star's strum of a guitar is overcome
by the mechanical-vibrato of the washers.

Condensation cuts dirt paths down
the glass door--hinges scream--a blast
of mouldering air slaps her face and melts
the mascara runnels Impasto-painted on her cheeks.

Soiled clothes are fed into the gaping mouth
of the machine as doves thrash against the ceiling.
How did she get here? Why did she come?
It's difficult to think past the thrum thrum thrum.

Near the vending automatics, flickering
like rapid-blinking eyes, a shape unfolds from the corner.
An old washerwoman begins to hum, the droning
of a thousand raging bees, or possibly, a mother's lullaby.

Outside the laundromat, lights slice the night,
a kaleidoscopic knife of red and blue. The hag licks
the leather of her lips and the keening truly begins.
The woman remembers now what she did.

The cry of the washer calls, and so the woman
goes to check her brood. There is blood in the water
just like in the tub of her children's bathroom.
It's difficult to think past the mum mum mum.

She places a coin in the dryer, takes a deep breath
before the ride. It is dark in the drum as the skin
is seared from her hide. She screams while
the washerwoman continues to sing,

never stops singing,

Please stop singing

for eternity.

— *Cecilia Dockins*

Call of the West

A giant sun blasts from the sky.
Beneath, rows of graves cover the parched earth,
A circular proscenium in the middle of the vast cemetery.

Just outside this graveled circle,
A tall man with long blond hair steps back.
Retreating shadows reveal wide scars across his sunburnt
skin;
He throws a shabby poncho over his shoulder in a single
motion.
As he moves from the heath,
In his right hand, a double-action pistol spits fire.

Beneath the skeletal, thorny branches of a massive
Mesquite tree
Stands a pudgy, brown-skinned man wearing an oversized
sombrero.
Bandoliers filled with silver bullets crisscross his bulging
chest,
His callused hands caked with dried blood and dirt
Grab the holstered revolvers at his sides, ready to kill;
His belly shakes with laughter as he takes aim at the
gringo.

Bullets bite into bark,
Shatter a cow skull into bone fragments,
Crack ancient stones to dust.

Buried in the shallow graves
Corpses of Civil War dead awaken -
Unamused, their teeth chatter like castanets.

Suddenly, between the two gun fighters,
A coffin pops out of the desiccated soil, a macabre jack-in-
the-box -
The bloated body of a bullet-ridden soldier slumps from
the open lid of the wreck;
Crawling masses of spiders and scorpions
Swarm from his slack-jawed mouth and empty eye sockets.

Across the western necropolis, a hot wind blows away
The echo of galloping horses,
The sound like cantina banter
Complaining that the high cost of the bounty
And its bonus of dead bodies
Just isn't worth the instructions
To the buried gold in the unmarked grave anymore.

— *Chad Hensley*

She Walks in Moonlight

Ice-scythed lyric, sharp enough
To bleed my frost-sheathed heart,
Jagged glacier, crimson within
The ruby-flowered caves

Concealing the unforgiven,
Ice-burned and wind-chilled memories
Of my own requiem, not in d-minor,
But in minor C, sharp, like my teeth

That pierced your pale-skinned veins,
The blue-streaked beauties of
Those bloody rivers within
Speckled shimmering, the Heavens,
The same sky the soul-destined
Heart beats for, beats for time

For patience, patience for Death,
For His cold-graved understanding,
Longing for the ghost-gloomed gaze
From His condescending eyes

Her moon-kissed luminosity whispers
        Kiss me with your living lips
                Worship me with your waning soul

Wandering pale amid Night's
Sleep-persuading sounds
Ethereal with sanguine purpose

But the lofty-aired breath
Is not made for immortality,
My sun-scorned love

For your ambivalent soul is destined
For neither starry Heaven
Nor fiery Hell.

— Clay F. Johnson

Forever and a Day

It's that phrase.

Forever and a day

The phrase I can't abide.

Forever and a day

Who wants to go beyond infinity?
Even one more day of pain?
Yet, the phrase subsists.

Forever and a day

With sing-song joy.

Forever and a day

The light hurts my eyes, you see,
and I can't feel my feet anymore.
One of his favorite phrases.

Forever and a day

Before he really gets to work.

Forever and a day

It will be the last thing I hear.
Soon, I hope.

It's just one more day.

– David C. Hayes

Playground

Forty-five years old:
Midway upon the journey… Perhaps.
Incurable optimist.

Playground in Desert Street
– Desolation City:
Once in a while I stop by.

Among children with huge eyes
Under a plaster sky, with my friend Raven
I rise and fall on the see-saw.

When Raven is up, I believe in Lovecraft's Gods.
When Raven is down, I regret a crucified carpenter.
In the middle, I feel a beautiful, terrible silence.

Huge-eyed children play among corpses of dead leaves.
While a Different Man walks outside the fence
Ordinary-Face People surround him, kicking, cutting,
biting.

Every wound has red lips.

A mouth begs mercy.
A mouth curses each god.
A mouth shouts animal verses.

A kick for the nose, a kick for the teeth
A kick for the balls and one for the ass.
A kick to break his back.

Sitting and chatting
Ordinary-Face People nibble a Different Man
One bite at a time.

A child, huge-eyed, approaches.
«Hey, man, I'm afraid.
Know someone to kick, to get over it?»

How they grow fast!» Says my friend Raven
flying away, leaving me alone
Surrounded by the children of Desert Street's playground.

— *Davide Camparsi*

Sutekh from the Throne

It starts with a sharp golden light —
this speaking in the dark jungle,
the needle-driven maelstrom
this knowing in the last lobe of the brain.

Just a little — a little mild excision
taking a lonely colonial drop
the memory of the ziggurat, the step
up the pyramid, the taste
of the blood in the heart.

Now all is as snow —
lost amongst the frozen wilderness.
Incision cleaving sight from memory
a tongue to speak, a lip to bleed.

It will all end in red desert.
Uncultivable, this severed member
silt and fish slime of the Nile
as it was in the beginning of our story:

He who wields the scalpel
rules the world
from his barren chamber,
every slice of Ausar
lessening everything.

A lone June bug
beating itself to death
on the floodlights
of the playing field

Forgetting in our truncated times
the all-important rolling
of the sun across the sky.

— Denise Dumars

Du Vieux Carre

There is no land like this.
It is a dreamscape lost, a battlefield grown over,
Echoing the spirits of soldiers, wounded and dying,
On a hardball maze.
It is a coliseum; lions and bears hide behind
Paint painted paint doors windowless and locked.

There are no dead today.
Still the bones decay in Number One, crypts tilting,
Corrupted by the sinking of reclaimed bayou
Paced apart by an ancient surveyor,
Marked with fading arrows buried shaft down.
And in Number One at One, an oven crypt,
A startled lithograph wrapped in plastic
Stares back above a water glass and floating crucifix.
At Three, Queen Marie is honored.
Plastic beads, squirrel's tail, two bricks wrapped in foil,
Her tomb is marked with brick etched crosses,
The drawing tools left over for the next convert.
And between the bricks, a white Fender Medium peeks out
With logo up.

I stooped to get it
And thought twice.
Dropped it face down
And will never forget.

On top of the tomb, sea birds fight over
A chicken bone and tufts of fur
Decorated with plastic flowers and red ribbons.
Daring the pushers,
Black women in white dresses
Form a procession for the dead.
They walk slowly, in step with a heartbeat,
For there are no dead today.

A black boy taps; his hat on the black boy top and
I can see him from a balcony above the street.
He spies me watching and points to his change.
I pitch him four quarters.
He scrabbles like a crab,
Bows low and forgets me.

The moon is full on Lake Pontchartrain
And the shrimp boats with their lights on are working.
It takes forever to travel from New Orleans,
Forever to cry for the dead.

— *Don Gillette*

The Parts We Don't Talk About

I am the unseen face just outside the dark window,
the one she doesn't want to believe in anymore.
Not the deliveryman or neighbor. Not even
the desperate result of a bad breakup.
I'm deeper than any of that.

I'm the fiend. The one who watched
and waited until she fell asleep to knock.
The one with the history of violence who
still makes her scream, "who's there?"
Even from outside I smelled her sweat,
sensed swirling panic in that shy, birdlike voice.

I almost laughed, but then she'd know:
I'm real. Under the skin. In the brain.
Hiding like a nasty virus no doctor can treat.
Look beneath the surface of her face,
where wrinkles etch sorrow and loss
and become all the things that terrify.

How the night amplifies a ghost, a memory!
A ringing phone, a shadow on the wall.
It's my grip that touches deeper than marrow,
my teeth that left those marks.
But I love her bones best, the solid frame
beneath tremors and twitches of muscle.
I've seen them once before and she knows,
they'll be mine again. Soon.

— E. F. Schraeder

Pain

She wore it like a cast-off shirt.
Loose, shapeless,
grimy at the collar and cuffs.
Threadbare and sun-bleached,
removing it only for care and inspection.
The tiny tears and holes she mended
with strong thread —
From the underside like a growing scab,
double-knotting and backstitching,
to re-enforce the seams.
And even to bed;
like armor as she traveled through Gehenna
to the Nothingness.
Where she leaves all memory of
past evils committed and borne —
Only to wake before dawn,
mind searching for hints of
What she tossed,
like collecting spilled dusting powder;
There's always some left over.
And the shirt is twisted tight around her neck
like a noose.

— Elsa Carruthers

Hitchhiker

The hitchhiking clown late for
his next appearance, balloon strings
clutched in his white gloved left hand,
thumb on right hand extended towards
the speeding traffic, beckoning to
the weekend travelers.

Your kids want you to stop
and pick him up, multi-colored
balloons reflected in their bright eyes.
Your wife wants you to pass him by,
already mad at you for not leaving
on time for the movie.

As for you? You're conflicted.

Ignore your wife, which will
have consequences later in bed; please
the kids, which will be construed as more
spoiling on your part; or heed the memory
of Killer Clowns From Outer Space
and Stephen King's, IT.

Airing on the side of caution,
you speed on by, the clown framed
in your rear view mirror lowering his
thumb and raising his middle finger,
sun glinting off the tip of a blood
stained butcher knife poking out
of his baggy, red sleeve.

– G. O. Clark

Bastet's Return

ENTOMBED HUNGER - AKH, KA

Spectral stone, striations gradient of shadowed truth
Split flat, fashioned into stained stone majesty,
Our window into frozen hearts bequeaths us colors
Buried under unseen time, uncovered, happy accident,
In violent strikes against a stock-still earthen mound;
In artifacts lie evidence of erstwhile tragedy,
Mere proof we sang unheard in time's stone wilderness.

Dig deeper down to find me.
Pull harder now to raise me to your light.
I am what devours your sacrifices.

ARTIFACT EN ROUTE - IB

So empty these days distance only creates echoes
Reach me where I wait grasping nothing anymore
Solid burns to smoke, ashes blow away, away

My chains ache

Clear horizon glimpsed through a slit between slats
Slivered hope served blind to either side may lurk
Vicious pouncing storms out there,
Out there away, away from what this is

My chains break

SPECTRAL FREEDOM - SHEUT

Each night, ride the owl.
Each day, sleep the dream.

What's real gets shredded
By talons of eternal now.

What's unreal quivers clear
On tips of bobbing branches.

Mists rise, trees shiver,
Small hearts jitter in fear.

Silent swoop of wings
Marks life with shadow.

Unexpected death digests flesh
Leaves bones in a skin sack.

Moments hours days lives:
Each night, ride the owl.

Each day, sleep the dream
Of night air rushing by.

CATFORM LURKING - BA, REN

Midnight cat with steel ball-bearing eyes
Golden glint of hissing hate
Darkness with claws unsheathed

Let dogs and jackals pass howling in the night
While at your hearth I await
Baby's breath-stealing indifferent death

Torpid, languid fate on silent feet
I drop dead offerings, beheaded
As an afterthought of malice

A purr to call forth demons
A growl to set forth rules

— Gene Stewart

A Daughter's Plea

You speak to me in whispers
of love and desire.
You tell me you can't wait
for the day of my arrival.
You never asked
me what I thought
of this life you are forcing
on me.
What of my desires? Or do they not matter
after all your attempts to capture me
to your plane of existence?
I was content where I was.
I did not need this life, nor want it,
but still you tried, until you succeeded.
The life you offer me is one of pain,
for I have seen it.
At ten I spend the night at my friend's
and her father makes us play games
with him that no little girl should
ever have to play.
At twenty I become pregnant
by a man I don't love and abort the fetus.
Why can't you be
so kind to me?
At thirty-three I give birth to a son
with down syndrome and at forty-one
kill him in a car accident and don't
grieve his loss, for I'll be free of his burden.
At forty-two I lose my sanity
my husband will have me committed
to lie with his assistant,
six years later I hang myself.
Could you not

be so selfish?
Could you save
me the pain that comes?
I hear your whispered words of desire
and a pat on the wall of my prison as
I loop the soft pulsing cord
about my neck and hope.

 — *J.P. Rosen*

Phantom Calls

Skin stretched arthritic hands
reach for the phone,
but it's not ringing.
Her whispered hello
leaves a question mark
suspended in air,
that hangs,
then slips away
like a smoke ring.
Disappointment smells like old tobacco.
Everyone gets one phone call, right?
Each time she passes the phone
she picks it up, puts it to her ear
waiting for a last sweet word.
From inside the house,
she reaches for the receiver again.
No answer. No ring either
but it doesn't stop her.
Any word will do.
The days creep along,
but she's tethered, tied,
within hearing distance of the possibility.
There's silence, stillness,
a slow weeping drip of blood
adding up, drop by drop
until there's a puddle
until there's a pond around her ankles
until there's river of blood
washing her out of the door
just as the phone rings.

— Janet Leach

Self-Portrait as Bad 1950's Science Fiction Movie

The ones where aliens represent communists,
or robots represent nuclear destruction?
Would you be The Giant Leech Woman or The Killer
Shrews?
King Dinosaur or The Night of the Giant Gila Monster?
Always some monster coming in to wreck
the girls in bikinis dancing to bongo drums
on towels on the beach, in barns in the country,
the tinny radio stating "Be on the lookout..."
turned down just as it describes the oncoming atrocity.
Kids driving down an empty interstate too fast
encounter the wreckage—spacecraft, collapsed bridge,
burned bodies. What apocalypse, specifically,
is created from radioactive astronaut and mutant
dinosaur, can you face with square-jawed sheriff
at your side? Think hard before you point your pistol,
the laser gun, before you set the dynamite or A-bomb
on the life forms unique and pitiful, stranded
upon your planet, wishing only for home.

— Jeannine Hall Gailey

Grandmother

disturbing
that one cloudy eye
even when its abhorrent nature falls
in the opposing direction

grandmother explains this is her gift
her way of seeing what dwells
behind the veil

there remains something else
something far more sinister
when her eye goes wide
and unblinking

whispering to ancestors
in foreign tongue
speaking of privileged things
revealed from beyond

still when that eye of hers swirls
with detritus misgivings
do I finally understand

grandmother does not belong to us
as she should
caught in the interim of life and death
as she is

nightly I pray
but only the wraiths return my pleas
while our god turns its back on us all.

— Joseph A. Pinto

Paranoid

I've always wondered
What's under my bed.
Or- what's in the closet?
Does it want me dead?
Did something creep into
My shoes overnight?
All of these thoughts
Just fill me with fright.
I wonder each moment
What lives in the shower.
I think about these
Scary things every hour.
I suspect the trash can
Contains something sinister.
And I fear for the safety
Of my little sister.
So, all of these places
I've tried to avoid.
And then people wonder
If I'm paranoid.

— Skye Caden

Bones.

Were swept.

Delicately. Some with gusto. Pushed and pulled. Guided home.
On wooden floors they don't rattle much,
but at 2am the sound is deafening.

I didn't mean to.

The box was there.

A million memories. And visually I was captivated. They tiptoed.
Snuck up on me they did,
and one extended index finger tapped on my shoulder.

They were all there.

In my tiny bedroom.

Somehow they broke the lock and made it past the kitchen,
through the living room, the foyer, and up the stairs.
Second room to the right.

And I lost my shit.

Tore them apart.

There were tears, femurs, metatarsals and metacarpals,
ribs and mandibles; it was a mess.
And when I was done dozens of hollowed eyes stared at me,
from decapitated dreams.

And I pulled out the broom.

And meticulously started my task.

Bones.

Were swept right back into the closet they escaped.
I didn't mean to call them out. It was the box, the same one
whose contents now light the fire in the living room.

It doesn't matter.

I can hear them rattling. Putting each other back together.
Isn't that what they do?
It's the haunt that always comes through.

Bones.

— *Jillian Rossi*

The Lady in White

I saw the lady gowned in white,
How ghostly white was she;
I met her of an autumn night,
Upon the misty lea.

A sorrow weighed upon her brow,
A sadness dimmed her eyes,
But she was lovely, I avow,
As Luna in the skies.

Her kiss was chilly on my cheek,
And cold her hand in mine
As through the woods we went to seek
Mnemosyne's dim shrine.

We found at last a sylvan grove,
And 'mid the autumn drift
A skeleton was interwove,
With mushrooms in each rift.

I turned to see her tearful face —
And yet the girl had gone,
Her spirit in its resting place
At scarlet crack of dawn.

And so I left her there to rest,
Beloved forevermore
Beneath the autumn leaves, where nest
The gnome and mandragore.

— *Kyle Opperman*

Burning Out

I reach to the light,
to its ethereal lure;
the smell of frankincense
buried over once again
by the must of earth.

It takes me again,
down into its acrid depths.
I can't hold my breath;
my screams dissolve into fog.
Will it take me now,
or will it play with its food
a little longer?

Or will I consume myself?

The fire smolders
and I lose myself in it.
I gasp for air,
reaching, retching;
just one more time, one more chance
to end this cycle.

It's now just a speck,
nothing left within reach;
hands clawing
through nothing
and then it is gone for good.

But I'm still here,
wherever that might be.
I've forgotten who I am.
It burns to ash,

and I breathe it out.
An exhale of spirit.
A cloud of broken dreams.

I've made my choice;
perhaps I'll die by it.
Or maybe,
just maybe,
I've enough breath left
to reach one last time
back up toward the light.

Or has it finally burned out?

— *Leigh M. Lane*

Alice After

It's been years since
she was swallowed deep
into that rabbit hole
but she still shudders
at solitaire and waits
for the red queen
to lop off her head.

Rats scuttle within
the china closet
rattling the crazed teapots
until their awful music
nearly drives her mad
and it's always twelve o'clock.

The Jabberwock's screams
remind her that nothing's real
and she weeps a bog of icy tears
that threatens to drown her
to pull her further into
this unending nightmare.

Jaundiced caterpillars crawl
through the red smoke
their hundred tiny claws
fastening in her brain
devouring her dreams.

She keeps a rabbit's foot by her bed
for luck, she says, as she grows
smaller and smaller
until her smile is all that's left
with its rows of desperate teeth.

— Lisa Lepovetsky

Bygones, Be Flygones: A Conversation with a Sarcophaga Flesh Fly

Please don't larviposition there!
As your sanguine compound mosaic orbits
Envelope my weakened, wasted form.
The symmetry of your gray and white motif's
Mesmerizing patterned hair design,
Comfort me, in this difficult time,
After seeing such a distorted self-image in your stare,
I'm too distraught to fight with my haunting new visage.

Its proper etiquette to ask, "May I?" before you colonize
me.
I try to relax or meditate in my foul and tattered clothes,
But those bristly black limbs so irritate with their
anchoring spurs.
Such persistent proboscis and maxillary pulps soak up a
lap, a taste
Of my essence, life force oozing from what's left of my
once Roman nose.
My hand is frozen still, inactive instead of routinely going
in for the kill.

Bold opportunist come join the party and feast.
Colonize your "proper host."
Since it's just you and me for now,
Let's make an amicable toast, "Bygones, be Flygones."
But in a week's time, a crowd abuzz.
After all, to you I'm just another beast or rotting piece of
meat.
Nourishing yourself by suckling my teat.

Lucky I'm not a Venus fly-trap but
A compassionate, once vegan,

Caring not to swat you away
For fear of causing you bodily harm.

Be it now, I'm a reluctant Zombie.
 I'll only limit myself to pick my bones and battles
 With animal eating human necrovores.

So, this is it, eh? The payback
For meat eating and fly swatting done so many years ago?
Your first instar larvae's spiracles libidinously
Fondle my flesh, orgasmically
Commence feeding immediately.
Inhabit what once was my nose
And down to the remains of
My once voluptuous chest.

All of our lives seem to be one big test.
Karma and nature seem to ultimately know best.

— *Lina Sophia Rossi*

(NB: Ref: for more on the flesh fly: http://
entnemdept.ufl.edu/creatures/misc/flies/
sarcophaga_crassipalpis.htm)

The Straw Man

His cornhusk feet
skitter
as he is dragged to the stake.
His drygrass arms
crackle
as they're tied.
His button eyes betray
nothing
when the torches come close.
Orange flame licks the viole(n)t night sky
as the others scream and wail.
Their fire:
       outrage
           pride
                certainty
                    bloodlust.
The poor demand justice.
The rich answer with silent smiles.
One at the back asks:
       "But..."
           "What if..."
                "Maybe..."
No one hears.
They can wait no more for satisfaction.
The fire is set.
Heat drives them back.
Smoke obscures vision.
And
so
no one sees the straw man's stitched mouth tear open
as he screams.

— Lisa Morton

day of the dead

The ground swelled
Writhing; stirred from underneath
as if by rambunctious earthworms
Or the tree roots were restless
Ill at ease with a case of nervous limbs at night
Tossing in a bed of dirt and blight

Cracks split the soil
and spindly talon-fingers reached forth
to scratch the surface; slice the crust
Like blades through the layers of ages
they clawed, birthed from nocturnal wombs
Scrabbling out of unearth'd tombs

Back to the light
in earnest stealth and stillness come
Their lids peeled off with groans
Up from the depths they swam
Droves of the departed, the dearly returned
Their state of rest now spurned

The weight of grime cast off
to pay a ghastly visit, hollow inside
The soulless flesh-and-bone remains
of untether'd spirits long since gone
Voyaging across a pit, a Black Sea of space
Leaving behind no physical trace

Neither human warmth nor kinship
Mere husks of decay that seek their fill
Risen from graves, smearing trails of rot
that painted the ground: a sluggish wake
Frightful, shambling in heartless decrepit hordes

While the living hammered boards

Baked loaves on tables abandoned
Pan De Muertos sitting cold and hard
Grown stale as the breathing cringed
at the sight of unwelcome guests —
Too appalled and distressed to break bread
upon "The Day Of The Undead"

No songs but grim dirges played
somber notes and marching beats
The hours hung heavy, thick and gray
Absent the color from celebrations
Subdued the festive cheer, affectionate cries
Only a hum of descending flies

Would this wave of corpses recede?
Once family or friends, reduced to ghouls
Estranged in the end and loathed
None wished to dance with the dead
These gaunt cadavers looked brittle, so weak
Wither'd to sticks, to figures bleak

Yet in dull murky eyes lurked a menacing glint
of famished cores and a vengeful dint.

— *Lori R. Lopez*

Wolf Waltz

"It's not kind," Red said
as she swung the cellar door
to the coal below. "It's not kind

to play with human hearts."
I wondered if her caution
was a mantra for herself

as though I still had fangs
as if she hadn't wrapped
sheep flay 'round my face.

"Watch out!" she shouted
"Those stairs won't hold!"
a moment before her shove

sent me tumbling, breaking
through every splintering
filthy rusted nail bristling

skin-ripping cracked board.
Yes, I thought, as my heart
spilled across the sooty floor,

yes, a sharp call:
it's not kind
not kind at all.

— *Lucy A. Snyder*

Night among the Dead: 1867

Amid the wounded were those who seemed dumb
and without understanding, but that is a thing
that I shove away inside with the rest of what
I've seen and done for the last five years.

And after this slaughter of women and children
the screaming horses, the gibbering of the maimed
dies down, sure as hell there will be a next time
and it will eclipse even this.

I'm drunk on weary and numb,
but I see her among the raped and dismembered,
she rises up as a ghost from the newly slain
and slips away into the prairie, dark hair afire
with the light of dying souls,

to where shadows rise and fall
into the tumbleweed and brush
when the faintest sounds of
scorpion-scuttle and snake-slither
can drive a man mad, if he's not yet there.

The wind shifts within the hour,
yucca flowers move and stygian bats arrive to suckle them.
Higher blows the wind and dust staunches the wet of my
wounds.
I get to my feet and stumble after that beautiful wraith

as the stars turn counterclockwise
to where the water holes are graced by ashen bones,
wondering if she'll be waiting for me
with arms stretched wide to take me in.

— Marge Simon

Health and Safety

This is how it begins: that loop of flex
could hook the foot. No wonder my eyes go
minesweeping the floor for trip-hazards, slip-
spills. The lead would insinuate itself
around my neck, wind tighter and tighter,
garrote. No, you can't afford to relax
a second. I spot the turned-up corner
of rug, the chrome and clear glass table
beyond. I've seen Final Destination
1 to 5. I know just how easily
these things happen. Death's just the other side
of the mirror. The phone sits with its arms
folded. The television has its mind on
other things. I know the audio books
talk about me. The door wants my fingers
in its hinges. The faulty iron hisses
and steams because it needs its livid imprint
on my chest. The shock could give one asthma
overnight. Stay back. See that kitchen knife?
I tell you, it wants my carotid artery
severed. The gas oven would like my head
on a baking tray. That toy dumper truck
on the stairs would double as a roller-
skate. See me cartwheel. Soon this building
will be fluttering, wreathed, with police tape.
Even your handbag is a booby-trap
set. While a whisky or two might calm the nerves,
everyone knows alcohol turns tragedy
to slapstick. Don't worry. I've made my peace.
I know exactly how this ends. I'll be
lucky if I make it out of here alive.

— *Mark Kirk bride*

When She Kissed Me

When she kissed me I felt so alive,
I felt every drop of blood course through my veins,
And a fire in my belly that grew and spread.
I could feel all of me. I could feel my toes and my scalp,
Her fingernails softly scratching the back of my neck
And sliding down my spine.

When she kissed me I felt my heart beat for her.
Through her lips came all the answers to all the questions
In the universe.
Or maybe the questions didn't matter anymore
As I fell into her mouth.

I needed her to hold me tighter, kiss me harder
As I parted my own lips, and her tongue filled my mouth,
And every part of me that was sex became engorged.
My body was hers, she could have it,
She knew it.

When she kissed me harder, her legs wrapping around my legs
Her fingers tangling in my hair
Her tongue slithered in my mouth while her teeth scraped my lips
And broke the skin.

I opened my eyes in the darkness
To look at her face, to fall into her eyes
But I saw in her eyes not the love and passion of a woman,

I saw graveyard dirt fall, I saw the worms crawl
Through the rotting bodies of men and women, all those
she'd kissed before me,
Bloodied, maimed, dead but alive,
Screaming from the hell that she'd locked them in.

I quickened, tasted blood and bile in my mouth,
Mine? Hers? Theirs? I didn't know,
But her lips stayed on mine as I tried to back away.
Her legs and her arms encircled my body,
How many legs? How many arms?
And even as I struggled to escape this monster,
As her teeth tore my flesh and her nails pierced my skin,
My body betrayed me, wanted her.

As she kissed me, I took one last look into those eyes,
Into her hell, to give me strength to break away,
But I was already hers, and I am inside of her hell.

I can sense her with another...kissing him.
I want to warn him to run, save himself, get away,
But I know by the time he hears my screams, our screams,
It will already be too late..

— *Megan Rhode*

Mister Deadsmile

On an April night when the air is cold,
when the wolves all sleep and shadows are bold,

when the moon never blinks its yellow eye

the wise ones say Mister Deadsmile is nigh.

He's waiting at the end of winding roads
looking for sinners to suffer his woes
like those who do wrong then run from their homes
heedless of fate and the horror it bodes.

That which confines him is compelled to free
this specter that malefactors can't flee,
baleful apparition tasting the breeze
and licking the scent of every sin's flea.

His grin as wide as a shark-filled shoreline
with eyes as black as a cadaver's brine,
his laughter an icy and shocking cry,
his touch, oh his touch, will chill and malign.

So think twice my children before you act,
committing transgressions, breaking the pact
then blindly flying until you are trapped
for Deadsmile is fingering your contract.

— Michael H. Hanson

Xiana's Skull

February,
and no rain falls,
just this shower of song
from our oak, the pines,
the neighbor's acacia,
full of nests and ivy.

They've found Xiana's skull
in the mountains, no body,
just the little bones
of a child's
severed head.

Birds know it's spring
long before we do,
and shock our breath away
with their sudden colors --
yellow, rust, cerulean,
the music of lust against gray,
word of coming summer,
the hope of better times.

It is an old and awful spell,
the young one lured
with promises of candy,
the carousel, a ride
on a friendly wolf's back

To a place where the sun shines,

wild sweet music
wakes her from bad dreams,
her mother, paroled,
kisses her hair,
she knows who her father is,
he has no knives,
and the birds sing all year.

— *Nancy Etchemendy*

Gratitude

Thanks for the flower that pleases my eye.
Thanks for the thorn that pricks my skin.
Thanks for the rope to hang me by.
Thanks for the fire to burn it in.

— Pete Mesling

Sweet Dreams, Love

"Sweet dreams, love," said daddy
Then he knelt and looked under the bed
"No monsters there"
Before checking the closet
"No monsters here."
He turned out the light,
Shut the door,
Slid home the bolt,
And latched the chain...

Ashley opened her eyes
Blinked once or twice,
Huddled in the blankets
She peeked over the sheets
Holding tight to her pillow
As the shadows surrounded her
Closer
Just a little closer
And closer still
So many shadows
Close enough to reach out
Touch
Caress
Claw their way into the pale moonlight
Filtering through the only window
The bars shadowed in long grey stripes across the floor
As Ashley blinked
Huddled
Peeked

Holding tight to her pillow
Until it, too, surrounded her
Closer
So very close

To scream, she'd have to open her mouth
But she'd learned long ago
The shadows and the pillow
Were only waiting for her to cry,
To open her mouth
And invite them in

So, in silence, Ashley blinked, huddled, peeked
As the shadows surrounded her
Burrowing inside with claws and bars and pillows
Until nothing remained but darkness
Silence
Loneliness
As Ashley blinked
Huddled
Peeked
And smiled
Flexing her claws
Baring her fangs
Waiting under the bed
In the closet
For daddy to return

— *Peter Adam Salomon*

Cryposo Woods in the Moonlight

A hint of a glint of a moonbeam kissed
the wings of those things in the midnight mist.
While they loop and they spin and they flutter about
to the cricket's chirp and the bullfrog's shout.
The dragonflies hover to cover their dance
and might join in, given half a chance.
The weeping willows sway in the breeze
waving "come on over" to the other trees
where the hoot owls hoot and the bats hang out
and the wolves unpack and the vultures pout.
There's a creeping crawler and slithering snake
and a lumbering giant thing, makes the ground quake.
The moon is their spotlight, the dark woods, their stage.
The night tells their story without one turned page.
There are quicksands where bone hands reach up towards
the sky
and under that boulder, a beast with one eye
tries to grab at your shoulder, or grasp for your throat
and rip out your screams before the second note.

A tentacled mass makes a pass and constricts
wrapping suction cup suckers, more pain it inflicts
as it feeds in the weeds on its unwary prey
then slithers back to its swamp, hidden away.
The howlers and growlers are out on the prowl
while perched on its bough sits the night watchman owl
who wonders aloud each character's name
so later he'll have some idea who to blame
for the cadaver curtain calls, dead body bows,

the carrion curtsies rigor mortis allows.
A slight touch too much of the vines in the wood
that entwine round your ankles and tangle up good
while the thorns and the briars, the nettles and burrs
prickling pokes at your skin 'til the burning occurs
and the itching and twitching and stinging begin.
Red rashes and welts start to blister your skin
but you can't scratch your itches, the vines wrap your wrists,
encircling your body with loops and tight twists
that cause you to swell up and blister and bleed
while you think that a scratching is all that you need,
but the vines climb your torso and more so, your throat;
make a red blistered necklace to match your neck bloat.
You don't hear the noise when the poison takes hold.
The swell and the smell of you, best left untold.

The moon very soon hides it pale face in shame.
Cryposo, at midnight has death in its name.
There's fur on the brambles and blood in the moss
from creatures whose features no one's come across,
like that huge hairy hump back with leathery wings
and scales on both tails with those hard spikey things.
Or that lady that soars through the night darkened sky
with the three rows of teeth and the third glowing eye,
screaming curses and cuss words and people's first names
like she's constantly livid at those whom she blames.
We've that two-headed imp with the really big feet
and his sister, Miss Twister whose breath smells so sweet
like a fresh batch of cookies all warm and delicious
but don't get too close 'cause she's really quite vicious.

She bit through the neck of the last one too close;
chewed off half of an ear and both lips and a nose.
The clouds wrap their shrouds round the shivering moon
and the night snuggles in, for the dawn's coming soon
so they slide in and hide in the darkness, the lairs,
or the caves, under rocks, in the trees, 'neath your stairs
or under the water or under the ground
they hide quietly without making a sound.
They wait for the night and the light of the moon
that they know will return and return very soon.

— *Randy D Rubin*

The Doppelgänger

You've seen me now. I noticed it,
The subtle jarring of your eye,
The look that lingered just a bit—
The flashlight of a startled spy.
You turned away, but I am here,
And just like you, I own a knife.
You know, that weapon that you fear?
And just like you, I own a wife.
She's different now, I do suppose.
I slashed her to a bloody mass.
I trimmed her ears and cropped her nose.
I dropped an eyeball in my glass.
When next we meet, my faithful twin,
I think, perhaps, I'll see your grin.

— *Richard Geyer*

The Killer Angels

I have seen the killer angels, in their war machines
as they bring our brothers home to God;
from battlefield red, full of lost hope and oblivion.

I have seen them in their glide paths,
removing life, tearing soul from body
with incredible pain, moment by moment, cell by cell.

And visages of hollow men
men who have done the macabre
and named it Legion.

Men who have tasted blood and found it sickly sweet,
who have smelt carrion and mourned their comrades,
lost to futility and silence and haunting memory.

My God, My God, forsake not the soldier,
he only does thy will, and your angels need not kill.

— *Richard Groller*

Another Match

The girl's aching hands grasp her last
Possession—a box of matches the size of a block
Of cheese with a sandpapery strip on one side.

She no longer fears the dark but snuggles
Inside it, letting it shield her from the memories in
The tiny brick room—especially that mess on the bed.

She sits in the far corner and tries ignoring
The relentless rain—which even down here sounds
Like tireless hammers—and the screaming wind.

The room smells of damp wood and fresh smoke.
She strikes another match.

The flame rises tall, then barely wavers.
She says, "Dad, I miss you so much."
He makes a long meal of the matchstick.

Father left to find help, though she begged him to stay.
She strikes another match.

The flame burns low and bluish yellow.
She says, "Brother, I hope it didn't hurt."
He fizzles out halfway down the stick.

Brother cried once before the storm gobbled him up.
She strikes another match.

The flame trembles like a wet kitten.
She says, "Mom, please come out of bed."
Mother mutely nips her fingertips.

She rattles her box — it stinks of sulfur
And unanswered prayers — and wonders who
Remains inside, waiting to play.

Rain pummels. Wind whispers.
The floor's cold. The walls sweat.
She strikes another match.

 — *By Rob E. Boley*

Prey

Childhood is a playground
shrouded in fog that thickens
with every passing year.
The chains of the empty
swing set rattle.
Who had been trying
to land on the moon?
I can't remember.
In dreams I navigate
through the haze
back to the church
with no name.
The crucifix atop the steeple
had been blackened
by a lightning strike,
it was said to be a blessing.
The breath of the swamp
spoiled the wood,
made it cry
with every step
across its warped surface.
I would hide my face
in my mother's hair
when the congregation
spoke in tongues,
and their eyes rolled back
in fanatic exaltation.
On Shrove Tuesday
the priest would call
the children to the alter
to mark a single forehead
with burnt palm.
I never wanted to be the one

who bore the cross.
I didn't question
when the chosen went missing
on Ash Wednesday,
the day of drums thundering,
smoke tattered on cypress;
the entire parish wearing white.
I wake up afraid,
mistaking my sweat
as the swamp's humid clutch,
my heart pounding
to a sacrificial beat.

— By Robert Perez

Monster's Doubt

The monster paused
claws deep in the warm,
red guts of the prey,
and wondered,
for the first time,
if it was all worth it.

Hide in dank, dark places
leap out to seize a two-legs,
tear it apart to
suck the life from its bones,
ram tentacles through its orifices,
feel energy drain until none was left.

What was the point?
What did it matter?
The monster was always alone.
The life, the energy faded. Another
two-legs had to be shredded.
The monster was still in the dark, looking out.

No, the monster thought.
I do what I do.
I do it well.
That has to be enough.
The monster drained the prey and
tossed it aside
slithered back into the dank and dark,
waited for the next.

— Robin Morris

Vigil

It's the sounds that get me
when the lights are low
the door half closed
and a wedge of honey-colored light
marks the floor

Soft-soled shoes whisper
as the nightshift make their rounds
low toned phones ringing
and the soft clatter of the keyboard
notes being taken, and orders updated

In our little box of time
there are the sounds of fluids dripping
filling the line stretched from pole to vein
and the hushed crinkle
of thin sheets
on your death bed

I try to think of better days
of movies and dinners
of walks in the mountains
photo albums filled with memories
fading, and so little when all is said and done

You were brash and outspoken
larger than life
now shrunken, diminished
a collapsing star
vanishing from sight

Hang on to every moment
even these last, bitter morsels

every recollection will be all that's left
when you're gone

Stale tinny air exhales from the vents
soft laughter from the desk in the hall
beyond the sealed windows
the horizon separates from the sky
it will be a cloudless day

One more night survived
but how many left?

I wait for you
one more shadow in the shadows
ghost at your bedside
while the tumor, bloated parasite
finishes its final meal

— *Rose Blackthorn*

Beauty in Death (Haiku)

Ford Mustang loses
Control, flips, rolls, ends in ditch
Creates modern art

— *Samson Stormcrow Hayes*

Dracula's Castle — Romania, 2015

The villagers had forgotten it
but not the storytellers.
Tourists visit

in search of a legend or haunting,
signs the Impaler's ghost is
tormented and taunting

foreign invaders who pry into the past
through heart-shaped peepholes watching
the undead trespass.

Our group hopes to capture the writer queen,
or a spectral visit from
entities unseen.

They say it was the inspiration
for Stoker's Gothic novel
our guide mentions,

"For the right price, you can rent the fortress.
Once, quite a well-known
Hollywood actress

paid for her family to stay overnight,
they heard voices, say they saw
a misty white light.

I don't like staying late here alone,
I've heard footsteps and knocking,
strange, hideous moans

and there's someone above racing

on a floor that doesn't exist,
as if they're chasing

prisoners or their prey, I swear on
my grandmother's grave, it
scares the shit—pardon

my English—out of me, and I didn't even
touch palinka, you know we locals
when drunk believe in

such monsters: strigoi, werewolves, Russia.
We'll drive a stake through those waking
from an alcohol-induced coma."

Then he led us to the torture chamber,
to a secret tunnel where
things became a blur

disoriented & dazed we crossed through
the passage behind the fire
where the Queen once flew

to meet her lovers under the moonlight
where they still wait, libidinous, for
one eternal bite.

— *Tausha Johnson*

Poets' Bios

Adrian Ludens is a short story author living in Rapid City, SD. You can find his work in: *Blood Lite 3: Aftertaste, The Mammoth Book of Jack the Ripper Stories, The Beauty of Death*, and many others. Visit Adrian at **www.adrianludens.com** for a cover gallery, blog, news, and more. Adrian is an Active member of the Horror Writers Association but writes in several genres. His newest collection, *When Bedbugs Bite*, is available on Amazon in a variety of formats.

Alessandro Manzetti is the Bram Stoker Award® winning author of more than twenty books in English and Italian, including works of fiction, poetry, and nonfiction. His poems and stories have appeared in numerous publications. His poetry collection *Venus Intervention* was nominated for the Bram Stoker Award (2014) and for the Elgin Award (2014, 2015). His volume *Eden Underground* was awarded the Bram Stoker Award (2015) His poems 'The man who saw the world' and 'Interiora II' were nominated for the Rhysling Award (2014, 2015). His new poetry collection *Sacrificial Night*, co-written with Bruce Boston, will be published in June 2015.Website:**www.battiago.com** .

Alex S. Johnson is the author of several books, including the official New Line Cinema spinoff novel *Jason X IV: Death Moon; The Doom Hippies, The Pit and the Void* and *Bad Sunset*. Also a music journalist who has published articles with *f* and *Metal Maniacs*, Johnson currently resides in Sacramento, California, where he owns and operates Nocturnicorn Books.

Angela Yuriko Smith publishes a monthly online newspaper by day (**PanhandleFocus.com**), blogs at *Dandilyon Fluff* (**dandifluff.com**) by night and writes fiction as often as possible in between. Her published works include fiction and nonfiction across multiple genres and she has been included in various anthologies and online publications. In the past she has served as a host for *JournalJabber* online radio talk show and has been interviewed on National Public Radio for her nonfiction work.

Annie Neugebauer is a novelist, short story author, and poet. She has work appearing in over fifty venues, including *Black Static*, *Apex Magazine*, and *Fireside*. Her book of poetry received an honorable mention in the Stevens Poetry Manuscript Competition by the National Federation of State Poetry Societies. She also has work forthcoming in anthologies such as *Suspended in Dusk 2*, *Fearful Fathoms*, and *The Beauty of Death*. Annie's the webmaster for the Poetry Society of Texas and a columnist for Writer Unboxed. She's represented by Alec Shane of Writers House. You can visit her at **www.AnnieNeugebauer.com** for blogs, poems, organizational tools for writers, and more.

Ashley Dioses is a poet of dark fantasy and horror from southern California. She is currently working on her first book of dark traditional poetry to be out from Hippocampus Press in 2017. Her poetry has appeared in *Weird Fiction Review, Spectral Realms, Weirdbook Magazine, Omnium Gatherum Media, Eye to the Telescope, Xnoybis, Necronomicum, Gothic Blue Book*, and elsewhere. Her poem, "Carathis", published in *Spectral Realms* No. 1, is mentioned in Ellen Datlow's full recommended *Best Horror* *of the Year Volume Seven* list.　She blogs at **fiendlover.blogspot.com**.

Bruce Boston is the author of more than fifty books and chapbooks, including the dystopian sf novel *The Guardener's Tale*. His poems and/or fiction have appeared in *Asimov's SF, Analog, Weird Tales, Strange Horizons, Daily Science Fiction, Realms of Fantasy, The Nebula Awards Showcase* and *Year's Best Fantasy and Horror*. His poetry has received the Bram Stoker Award, the *Asimov's* Readers Award, the Gothic Readers Choice Award, the Balticon Award, and the Rhysling and Grandmaster Awards of the SFPA. His fiction has received a Pushcart Prize, and twice been a finalist for the Bram Stoker Award (novel, short story). **www.bruceboston.com**.

Cecilia Dockins lives in Tennessee and spends most of her time wrangling words and parrots. She is a graduate of the Odyssey Writing Workshop. Her fiction has appeared in *Sanitarium Magazine, HWA Poetry Showcase Volume 1*, and various anthologies. For more about Cecilia, check out her website at **www.ceciliadockins.com**.

Chad Hensley is a Bram Stoker Award-nominated author who had his first book of poetry *Embrace the Hideous Immaculate* published in May of 2014 from Raw Dog Screaming Press (available at the publisher's website and Amazon.com). His recent poetry appearances include *Weirdbook* issues #31 and #32, the first five volumes of S.T. Joshi's *Spectral Realms* published by Hippocampus Press, *Space and Time* #122, *Weird Fiction Review* #5 published by Centipede Press, and *The Pedestal* Magazine.com issue #74. His short story "A Brush of Mammoth Wings" and poem "The Call" appear in *Nightgaunt* #3 in both French and English.

Chad Stroup received his MFA in Fiction from San Diego State University. His work has been featured in anthologies like *Splatterlands* and *Creature Stew,* and his poetry also appeared in the first two volumes of the HWA Poetry Showcase. *Secrets of the Weird*, Stroup's debut novel, is forthcoming from Grey Matter Press. Visit Subvertbia, a home for some of his short fiction, poetry, and reviews at **http://subvertbia.blogspot.com/**, and drop by his Facebook page as well. **https://www.facebook.com/ChadStroupWriter**.

Clay F. Johnson is an amateur pianist, soi-disant adventurer, devoted animal lover, chronic insomniac, and incorrigible reader of Gothic literature and Romantic-era poetry. Among other literary endeavors, he is currently working on a small collection of poems and short stories inspired by the haunting events that took place in the "year without a summer" of 1816 that gave birth to Mary Shelley's *Frankenstein*, Byron's *Fragment of a Novel* and *Darkness*, and Polidori's *The Vampyre*. Find out more at **http://clayfjohnson.blogspot.com/**.

Corrine De Winter. Nominated four times for the **Pushcart Prize**, Corrine De Winter's poetry, fiction, essays and interviews have appeared worldwide in publications such as the *The New York Quarterly, Yankee, Sacred Journey, Fate*, and over 900 other publications. She has been the recipient of awards from Triton College of Arts & Sciences, *Writer's Digest*, The Esme Bradberry Award, The Madeline Sadin Award, The Rhysling Award, The Bram Stoker Award, and has been featured in *Poet's Market* 1995-2016. Ms. De Winter is a member of HWA (Horror Writer's Association), and the founder of **SMALL WORLD FUND FOR CHILDREN.** De Winter is the author of 9 collections of poetry & prose including *Like Eve, The Half Moon Hotel,* and

Touching The Wound, which sold over 3000 copies in its first year, *The Women At The Funeral,* winner of the 2004 Bram Stoker Award for superior achievement in poetry, and *Tango In The 9th Circle* (Dark Regions Press), the Bram Stoker Award nominated *Virgin of the Apocalypse* and *Venus Intervention.*

David C. Hayes is an author and performer. His films, like *A Man Called Nereus, Bloody Bloody Bible Camp, Dark Places* (and approximately 60 more) can be seen worldwide. He is the author of several novels, collections and graphic novels including *Cherub, Cannibal Fat Camp, Scorn* and *Muddled Mind: The Complete Works of Ed Wood, Jr.* As a playwright, his plays have been produced from coast to coast with a run Off-Broadway for the comedy *Swamp Ho.* Visit him online at **www.davidchayes.com**.

Davide Camparsi lives in Verona (Italy), where he works as an architect. In 2013 he started to participate in literary competitions: "Perché nulla vada perduto" won the XIX edition of Trofeo RILL. "Se Dio è amore" won the ESESCIFI contest. "Cuordrago" won the Trofeo La Zona Morta 2014. "Sotto il mare la Montagna sogna" was chosen to open the anthology *L'Universo di Lovecraft.* In 2015 "La pecora perduta" was included in "Ma gli Androidi mangiano spaghetti elettrici?" of Eatalian Sci-Fi for EXPO; "Fenditure" won the weird-horror competition by Esecranda; the novel *Terreno di sepoltura* won the Premio Horror Polidori.

Denise Dumars' latest book of supernatural horror poetry, *Paranormal Romance: Poems Romancing the Paranormal*, was nominated for the Suzette Haden Elgin award. She is currently looking for representation for *Page of Swords*, a Gothic romance novel she co-authored with Corrine De

Winter. Denise lives in one of L.A.'s beautiful beach cities, but her heart is in New Orleans.

Don Gillette has been writing since he asked for (and received) one of the original "Tom Thumb" typewriters for his 6th birthday. He is the author of two novels, dozens of short stories and poems, and hundreds of newspaper and magazine articles. He is a retired Army National Guard Chief Warrant Officer Four and served on Active Duty during Operations Desert Storm and Desert Shield. Don was born and raised on the Atlantic Coast and currently lives in Nashville, Tennessee, with his wife, Sim Yoon.

E.F. Schraeder's creative work has appeared in journals and anthologies including *Dark Moon Digest, Bloodbond, Voluted Tales, Hoax, Haz Mat Review, Carnival of the Damned, The Kennedy Curse, Petals in the Pan*, and others. As well as authoring a poetry chapbook, *The Hunger Tree*, Schraeder's nonfiction has been included in the anthologies *Queering Sexual Violence* and *Kicked Out*. Schraeder studied ethics and the humanities in graduate school, has an interdisciplinary Ph.D. in social philosophy, and teaches as an adjunct lecturer. Additionally, Schraeder contributes to an animal advocacy webcomic (**clawtheory.com**) and is online at **www.efschraeder.com**.

Elsa Carruthers lives in California with her family. She is a treasure trove of useless facts and is convinced she was born in the wrong time. When she's not writing, Elsa enjoys piping hot cups of cocoa and talking to herself. Elsa graduated from Seton Hill University's MFA program for Writing Popular Fiction. She has published in several anthologies and is hard at work on her poetry and revising her first novel.

Gene Stewart has traveled the world but is quartered currently, or bivouacked perhaps, if floods continue, in the American Midwestern Wilderness, where he continues researching and writing. More about him can be found at **genestewart.com/wordpress**.

G. O. Clark's writing has been published in *Asimov's Science Fiction, Analog, A Sea Of Alone: Poems For Alfred Hitchcock, Spectral Realms, Horror Zine, Daily SF* and many other publications. He's the author of eleven poetry collections; the most recent is *Gravediggers' Dance*, 2014, Dark Renaissance Books. His second collection of fiction, *Twists & Turns*, came out in 2016 from Alban Lake Publishing. He won the Asimov's Readers Award for poetry in 2001, and was a Bram Stoker Award finalist in 2011. He's retired, and lives in Davis, CA. See **http:// goclarkpoet.weebly.com/** for more info.

Janice Leach has edited three volumes of *Quick Shivers* from **Dailynightmare.com**. She is co-author along with her partner of a volume of poetry, *Til Death*, coming from Raw Dog Screaming Press in 2016.

Jeannine Hall Gailey served as Redmond, Washington's second Poet Laureate. She's the author of five books of poetry: *Becoming the Villainess, She Returns to the Floating World, Unexplained Fevers, The Robot Scientist's Daughter*, and *Field Guide to the End of the World*, winner of the Moon City Press Book Prize. Her work has been featured on NPR's *The Writer's Almanac*, Verse Daily, and in *The Year's Best Fantasy and Horror*.

Jillian Rossi is an American author of horror, supernatural fiction, science fiction and fantasy. She is a full time mom, RN and writer. She enjoys saving lives, shiny objects, kilts, gaining minions, chasing ghosts (or running from them...mostly running) and carrying salt and chalk on her at all times. She currently lives in the South Bay with her family and son.

Joseph A. Pinto is the author of two published books — the poignant novella *Dusk and Summer* and the horror novel *Flowers for Evelene*. His unique voice has been showcased in a multitude of anthologies and magazines as well as individually published short stories. Joseph, who resides in New Jersey with his wife and daughter, is a member of the HWA as well as the co-founder of Pen of the Damned (**penofthedamned.com**). You can find additional works by Joseph on his personal blog at **JosephPinto.com**, follow him on twitter as @JosephAPinto, and friend him on Facebook.

J.P. Rosen is a speculative fiction writer and poet who lives in the Pacific Northwest. He explores the darkness in the world through his writing. He writes dark poetry, short fiction, and an occasional novel. He is a supporting member of the Horror Writers Association and a member of the Science Fiction Poetry Association. For a free short story go to **http://jprosen.com/hwa-poetry**.

K. A. Opperman is a traditionalist poet of horror and dark fantasy from Southern California. He has been/will be published in such venues as *The Weird Fiction Review, Spectral Realms, Nameless Magazine, Weirdbook, Gothic Blue Book, The Audient Void*, and many others. His book length Weird poetry collection, *The Crimson Tome*, came out last year from Hippocampus Press. He is an Affiliate Member of the HWA, and a member of the SFPA.

Kathryn Ptacek's novels are now out as ebooks from Crossroad Press and Necon Ebooks. Her first collection of short stories, *Looking Backward in Darkness*, was released by

Borgo Press in 2013. Also, she has short stories in three recent anthologies: *Fright Mare, Expiration Date*, and *Fright Mare-Women Write Horror*. Kathy lives in rural northwest New Jersey and shares her old Queen Anne home with lots of books, the requisite author cats, unusual teapots, and the occasional visiting mouse. She can be reached at **gilaqueen@att.net** or through her Facebook pages.

Lina Sophia Rossi is a writer, photojournalist and was editor of various publications in high school, university and beyond. Her poems were published in SUNY Stony Brook's Italian Literary magazine, *Voci*. In addition to being a biologist, anthropologist and electron microscopist, she presently works as a family physician where she goes by her birth name, in a supposedly haunted state asylum. She is also the communication chair and delegate of the hospital's state employees association. Her debut novel manuscript, still in an editor's hands, was successfully pitched at the World Horror Convention in Atlanta, so stay tuned.

Leigh M. Lane. In addition to writing dark speculative fiction for over twenty-five years, Leigh M. Lane edits for the Cerebral Writer, dabbles in the fine arts, holds a third-degree black belt in karate, has sung and written for bands ranging from classic rock to the blues, and once sang the National Anthem for the opening of a Dodger's game. She holds a degree in English, having graduated from UNLV magna cum laude. She currently lives in the dusty outskirts of Sin City with her husband, an editor and educator, and one very spoiled cat.

Lisa Lepovetsky has published both poetry and fiction in the dark fantasy, horror and mystery genres, in both magazines (*Bete Noire, The Pedestal, Disturbed Digest, EQMM*, and many others) and anthologies (*Grails, Blood*

Muse, Dark Destiny, etc.) and a paranormal novel, *Shadows on the Bayou*. She earned her MFA from Penn State, and has frequently taught writing and literature classes for them and the U. of Pittsburgh. Her most recent book is *Voices from Empty Rooms* from Alban Lake.

Lisa Morton is a screenwriter, author of non-fiction books, award-winning prose writer, and Halloween expert whose work was described by the American Library Association's *Readers' Advisory Guide to Horror* as "consistently dark, unsettling, and frightening". The author of over a hundred published short stories and four novels, her most recent releases include *Ghosts: A Haunted History* and the short story collection *Cemetery Dance Select: Lisa Morton*. She can be found online at **http://www.lisamorton.com**.

Lori R. Lopez dips her pen in poetry, prose, and art. Her books include *The Dark Mister Snark, Poetic Reflections: The Queen of Hats, Odds and Ends: A Dark Collection*, and *Chocolate-Covered Eyes*. Lori's work has appeared in the strangest of places: on Hellnotes and Halloween Forevermore; in *The Horror Zine, Weirdbook*, and *The Sirens Call,* as well as numerous anthologies including the *H.W.A. Poetry Showcase Volume II, Journals of Horror: Found Fiction*, and *Dead Harvest*.

Lucy A. Snyder is a five-time Bram Stoker Award-winning writer. Her poetry will soon appear in *Asimov's Science Fiction* and *Scary Out There* and has appeared in *Nightmare Magazine, The Cutting Room, Weird Tales*, and *Strange Horizons*. Her books include the novels *Spellbent, Shotgun Sorceress*, and *Switchblade Goddess*, the nonfiction book *Shooting Yourself in the Head For Fun and Profit: A Writer's Survival Guide*, and the collections *While the Black Stars Burn, Soft Apocalypses, Chimeric Machines*, and *Installing Linux on a Dead Badger*. She lives in Columbus, Ohio and teaches in Seton Hill University's MFA program in Writing Popular Fiction.

Marge Simon lives in Ocala, Florida and is married to Bruce Boston. She edits a column for the HWA Newsletter, "Blood & Spades: Poets of the Dark Side," and serves as Chair of the Board of Trustees. She won the Strange Horizons Readers Choice Award, 2010, the SFPA's Dwarf Stars Award, 2012, and the Elgin Award for best poetry collection, 2015. She has won the Bram Stoker Award® for Poetry, the Rhysling Award and the Grand Master Award from the SF Poetry Association, 2015. She has work in *Chiral Mad 3* and *Scary Out There* anthologies, 2016. **www.margesimon.com**.

Mark Kirkbride lives in Shepperton, England. His debut novel *Satan's Fan Club* is published by Omnium Gatherum. His poetry has appeared in the *Big Issue*, the *Morning Star* and the *Mirror*.

Megan Rhode is an editor in her day job and a writer at night. She lives in Studio City with her little black cats, who keep her demons at bay. But every once in a while, a demon gets past her cats, and Megan has to trap it inside a poem or a story.

Michael Arnzen holds four Bram Stoker Awards and an International Horror Guild Award for his disturbing (and often funny) poetry, fiction, and other literary experiments. He holds a PhD in English from University of Oregon and teaches in the MFA program in Writing Popular Fiction at Seton Hill University. Raw Dog Screaming Press recently published the 20th Anniversary edition of his first novel (*Grave Markings*), along with a decade-long collection of his micropoetry (*The Gorelets Omnibus*), and will be releasing his new nonfiction study,

The Popular Uncanny, this October. See what he's up to now at **gorelets.com**.

Michael H. Hanson is the Creator of the Sha'Daa shared-world, horror/fantasy anthology series currently consisting of *Sha'Daa: Tales of The Apocalypse, Sha'Daa: Last Call, Sha'Daa: Pawns, Sha'Daa: Facets*, and the soon to premiere *Sha'Daa: Inked*, all published by Moondream Press (an imprint of Copper Dog Publishing LLC). He has had three collections of poetry published: *Autumn Blush* and *Jubilant Whispers*, whose second editions will soon be published by Racket River Press (an imprint of Copper Dog Publishing LLC), and *Dark Parchments: Midnight Curses and Verses* released by Moondream Press on Halloween 2015.

Nancy Etchemendy's novels, short fiction, and poetry have appeared regularly for the past 30 years, both in the U.S. and abroad. Her work has earned a number of awards, including three Bram Stoker Awards and an International Horror Guild Award. *Cat in Glass and Other Tales of the Unnatural*, her collection of short dark fantasy, was named an ALA Best Book for Young Adults. She lives and works in Northern California where she leads a somewhat schizophrenic life, alternating between unkempt, introverted writer of weird tales and gracious (she prays) wife of Stanford University's Provost.

Peter Adam Salomon's debut novel, *Henry Franks*, was published in 2012. His second novel, *All Those Broken Angels*, was nominated for the Bram Stoker Award for Superior Achievement in Young Adult fiction. Both novels were named a 'Book All Young Georgians Should Read' by The Georgia Center for the Book. His short fiction has appeared in numerous anthologies and his poem 'Electricity and Language and Me' appeared on BBC Radio

6 performed by The Radiophonic Workshop in December 2013. Eldritch Press published his first poetry collection, *Prophets*, in 2014 and Bizarro Pulp Press will publish *Pseudopsalms: Saints V. Sinners* in 2016. He was the Editor for the first books of poetry released by the Horror Writers Association, *Horror Poetry Showcase Volumes I* and *II*. He is a member of SCBWI, HWA, SFWA, SFPA, ITW, and The Authors Guild and is represented by the Erin Murphy Literary Agency.

Pete Mesling's debut collection of short fiction, *None So Deaf*, is currently available from Books of the Dead Press. Other publishing highlights include selling a story to Mort Castle, and having it appear alongside a reprint of Clive Barker's "Midnight Meat Train," as well as working directly with the late Richard Matheson on an online retrospective about his career in film and television. Mesling has also sold fiction to such publications as *All-American Horror of the 21st Century* and, most recently, the *Spawn of the Ripper* anthology from April Moon Books. He is hard at work on his first novel.

Randy D. Rubin is a proud member of HWA and a writer of dark fiction and even darker poetry. His first poetry collection, *The Demon in my Head Doth Speak*, was published last year and his dark poem "Changing Channels" was included in 2015's *HWA Poetry Showcase*. Randy D. has been likened to the Dr. Seuss of Horror Poetry. His next poetry collection, called *The Joint,* will be published by EMP Press in the highly anticipated, *The Prison Compendium* due out in November 2016. Look for Randy D.'s first collection of short stories to come out in August.

Richard Geyer operates Phantom-Wooer: The Thomas Lovell Beddoes Website and is a librarian at Adrian

College in Michigan. Brown University has been collecting his self-published chapbooks of poetry for its Harris Collection of American Poetry and Plays since 2001. *The Madhouse Poems of Richard Creech*, which contains all of the poems from his first nine chapbooks of poetry, is available from Amazon. His tenth and most recent poetry collection, *Richard Creech Rises Again*, is available from Lulu. Geyer edited the poetry journal *Contemporary Rhyme* from 2004 to 2008. Visit his website at **http://www.richardgeyer.com**.

Richard Groller is co-author of *The Warrior's Edge*, a contributing author to *The American Warrior*, and published in such venues as *Military Intelligence, The Field Artillery Journal, Guns & Ammo*, and the *Journal of Electronic Defense*. He is published in the *Heroes in Hell* series (6 volumes) and in the horror anthology *What Scares the Boogeyman?* from Perseid Press. He is published in the IronClad Press horror anthology *Terror by Gaslight* and by Moondream Press in two volumes of the *Sha'Daa: Tales of the Apocalypse* series and *The Book of Night*, an illustrated book of macabre poetry he edited.

Rob E. Boley grew up in Enon, Ohio, a little town with a big Indian mound. He later earned a B.A. and M.A. in English from Wright State University in Dayton, Ohio. He's the author of THE SCARY TALES series of dark fantasy novels featuring mash-ups of classic fairy tale characters and horror monsters. His fiction has appeared in *Pseudopod, Clackamas Literary Review*, and *Best New Werewolf Tales*. He lives with his daughter in Dayton. Each morning and most nights, he enjoys making blank pages darker. You can get to know him better at **www.robboley.com**.

Robert Perez. Robert Perez's earliest memory is of death. Okay- so maybe it was just crawling around the couch and looking up at an inflatable ghost, but horror has always inhabited the dark corners of his mind. He lives halfway between reality and fantasy at all times. His poem, "The Man Who Disappears", was published in the *HWA Poetry Showcase Volume II*, his poems, "Eight Arms To Hold", and "Hungry Moon", were published in *The Literary Hatchet Vol.13*, and his poem "Sweet Dreams" was recently published in *The Literary Hatchet Vol.14*. Follow @TheLeader on twitter to keep up with future projects.

Rose Blackthorn lives in the high mountain desert with her boyfriend and two dogs, Boo and Shadow. She spends her time writing, reading, being crafty, and photographing the surrounding wilderness. She is a member of the HWA and her short fiction and poetry has appeared online and in print with a varied list of anthologies and magazines. Her first poetry collection *Thorns, Hearts and Thistles* was published in February 2015, and the novelette *Called to Battle: Worthy Vessel* was published in October 2015. More information can be found at **http:// roseblackthorn.wordpress.com/**.

Samson Stormcrow Hayes—Author of the critically acclaimed graphic novel *Afterlife* (YALSA quick picks selection), screenwriter of *The Deal*, a ghost writer on a Steven Seagal film (advance apologizes if you've seen it, I was following the producer's instructions), and author of numerous stories and poetry. Hayes has written for Nigel Lythgoe (producer of *American Idol*), *The Weekly World News*, and his epic epitaph. Originally from Cleveland, Ohio, he now resides in Los Angeles where he expects the smog to slowly kill him. He can be found in old parking lots, abandoned malls, or at **www.Stormcrowhayes.com**.

Skye Caden is an avid reader and writer. Skye enjoys writing poetry and short fiction. When not writing, Skye's other interests and hobbies include entomology and political science. Skye's goals include a career in acting and political activism.

Tausha Johnson is part ghost whisperer, part Cherokee. She received her MFA at St. Andrews (Scotland) and a BA in Literature from UC Berkeley. Her prose and poetry have appeared or are forthcoming in various online and print publications, including *Folk Horror Revival: Corpse Roads, Haikuniverse, HWA Poetry Showcase 2, Danse Macabre* and *Best of Vine Leaves Literary Journal*, among others. She currently lives in the countryside of Spain, but sometimes surfaces as the program director for The Horror Writers Workshop in Transylvania. You can channel her here: **http://killyourdarlingswriter.com/**.

www.ingramcontent.com/pod-product-compliance
Lightning Source LLC
Chambersburg PA
CBHW070456130626
46555CB00003B/1032